KT-379-471

....

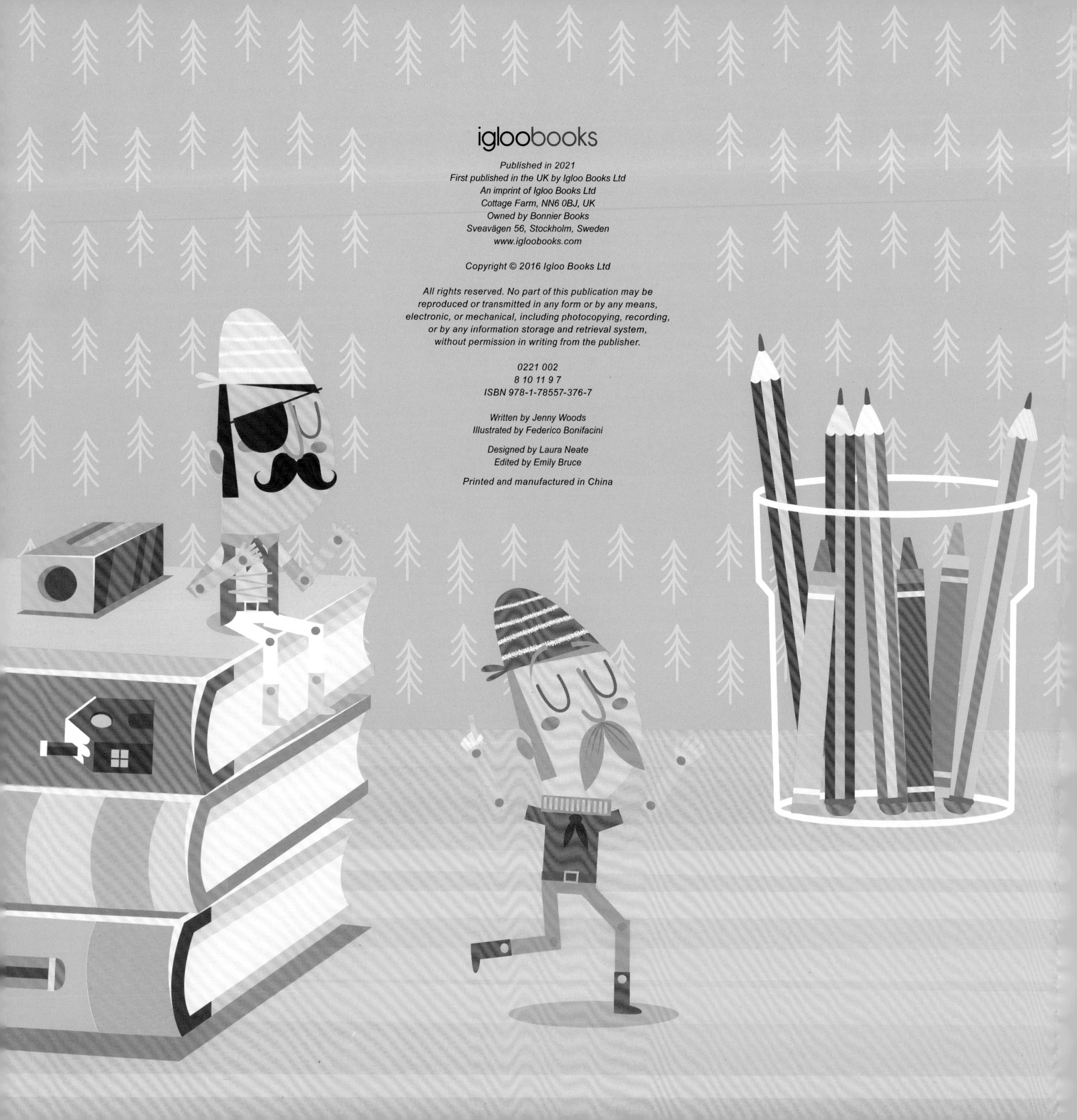

igloobooks

Published in 2021
First published in the UK by Igloo Books Ltd
An imprint of Igloo Books Ltd
Cottage Farm, NN6 0BJ, UK
Owned by Bonnier Books
Sveavägen 56, Stockholm, Sweden
www.igloobooks.com

Copyright © 2016 Igloo Books Ltd

All rights reserved. No part of this publication may be reproduced or transmitted in any form or by any means, electronic, or mechanical, including photocopying, recording, or by any information storage and retrieval system, without permission in writing from the publisher.

0221 002
8 10 11 9 7
ISBN 978-1-78557-376-7

Written by Jenny Woods
Illustrated by Federico Bonifacini

Designed by Laura Neate
Edited by Emily Bruce

Printed and manufactured in China

TOY TROUBLE

igloobooks

There was a lot of noise coming from 23 Blossom Drive.
It's not fair! I never get invited to the dolls' tea parties.
We don't get to play on the pirate ship.
Or drive the fire truck.

The children had gone away and the toys were arguing.
I'd just like to visit the fairy castle.

Suddenly, Fairy Fifi whooshed past on a big rocket, with a crew of fairies waving from the window.
VROOOM!
We can do what we like while the children are away!

In that case, I'm getting changed.
This spacesuit is itchy and the helmet is messing up my hair!
Spaceman Sam put on a sparkly jacket and a cowboy hat.
WANTED
Perfect!

You can't wear that!
A spaceman has to wear a spacesuit.
But Sam took no notice of Teddy. He was too busy admiring his new outfit in the mirror.

So Teddy tried to stop the fairies instead.
Go back to the castle!
But the fairies wouldn't listen.
Worn out, Teddy flopped down on a chair.

MOOOVE!
I'm getting my hooves polished and you're in my seat.
What are the farm animals doing in the beauty salon?

We're being pampered.
And getting fabulous new hairstyles.
Teddy tried to herd the farm animals back to the barn, but they refused to go.

Stomping out of the salon, Teddy almost crashed into a unicorn pulling a golden carriage full of soldiers.

It clattered to a stop, sending the soldiers tumbling to the floor.

Where's your tank?
This carriage is much nicer.
It's got a mini fridge and a disco ball.
Did someone mention a ball?

Captain Crossbones clambered down the rigging of the toy ship, followed by Scurvy Sue and a band of fearsome pirates.
I've always wanted to go to a ball.
Me too!
Let's hold one at the fairy castle.

Teddy shouted and stomped his feet, but the toys were much too excited to listen.

The dancing pirates leapt out of the way as a police car pulled up, its sirens wailing loudly.

The policemen turned on their flashing lights and led the toys into the fairy castle.

Teddy sat in the toy box feeling fed up.
He could hear music and laughter coming from the ball.
Perhaps I'd better go and keep an eye on things.

At the fairy castle, the dance floor was crowded with toys of all shapes and sizes showing off their dance moves.
It looked so much fun that Teddy couldn't resist joining in.

Teddy waved his paws in the air as he bopped and boogied to the beat. He didn't hear the sound of footsteps outside the playroom door, or hear the toys shout...

STOP DANCING!

The children are back!
Teddy froze in the middle of a twirl.
Quick! Tidy up!
Frantically, the toys put everything back in place. Well, almost everything!

Suddenly, the door swung open and the children ran into the playroom.
What's happened?
This isn't how we left it.
Teddy held his breath.

Mummy must have tidied and mixed up all the toys!
It's given me a great idea for a new game!

Now we can all try something different!